T0196529

ASSASSIN'S
UNCERTAINTY

ASSASSIN'S
UNCERTAINTY

MACEY CAMP

ASSASSIN'S UNCERTAINTY

iUniverse books may be ordered through booksellers or by contacting:

iUniverse
1663 Liberty Drive
Bloomington, IN 47403
www.iuniverse.com
1-800-Authors (1-800-288-4677)

Because of the dynamic nature of the Internet, any web
addresses or links contained in this book may have changed
since publication and may no longer be valid. The views
expressed in this work are solely those of the author and do
not necessarily reflect the views of the publisher, and the
publisher hereby disclaims any responsibility for them.

Any people depicted in stock imagery provided by Getty Images are
models, and such images are being used for illustrative purposes only.
Certain stock imagery © Getty Images.

ISBN: 978-1-5320-5540-9 (sc)
ISBN: 978-1-5320-5541-6 (e)

Print information available on the last page.

iUniverse rev. date: 08/30/2018

Dedicated to my late grandmother Kris Camp, the rock and support of my family.

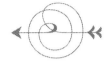

CHAPTER ONE

Kiera

The clock was ticking as I ran through the streets. I had to get to the palace soon or I would fail the mission.

"All hail King Austin!" The crowd shouted. It was summer solstice, which had everyone celebrating in the streets. Tonight would be the biggest party of the year. It would also be the night where King Austin would be killed, by me.

I pushed to get through the crowd. There had to be millions of people on the street. Having observed this city for two weeks I knew the street rarely had this many people on it.

The horns announced the coming royals. I had to hurry I'm supposed to be in the throne room before the party began. I looked at a tower where a gigantic clock was. I had 15 minutes.

Creeping along the palace walls I searched for a place to crawl over without being seen. Finally I found a place in the wall where bricks were missing. *Perfect for climbing* I thought to myself.

"Can I help you?" A deep, rich voice said from behind me. I turned around only to collide into the guys chest.

"Hello prince aren't you supposed to be celebrating?" I purred.

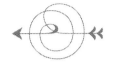

CHAPTER TWO

Cody

"I should ask the same of you." I looked the girl up and down. She certainly wasn't dressed to celebrate. She wore dark clothing with a solid black cloak.

I escaped the sufferable crowd to get some fresh air when I noticed her.

"What I do is none of your business." She hissed.

"Technically everyone is my business since this is my kingdom." I grinned, hoping to see a smile on her grim face.

There was no such luck as she said, "This isn't your palace yet." I rolled my eyes.

Usually girls would be head over heels with my smile but not this one.

"What are you doing anyway?"

"Needed to take a break from the crowd." Was all she said and walked away from me. No one had ever acted that way to me which made me all the more curious about her.

CHAPTER THREE

Kiera

Thanks to the prince I had to find another way to get in. I had 2 minutes before my scheduled time to kill the King of Herrington. Finally I found another place in the wall where bricks were missing. It took only a few seconds to climb over and run across the courtyard. Sneaking into the palace was a bit harder since there were sentinels every few yards but blending into the shadows was easy thanks to my dark clothing. Within seconds I was standing outside of the throne room. A glance at my watch showed I had a minute left before people were supposed to be let in.

"Fancy seeing you again." The Prince's voice came from behind me. I sighed inwardly in frustration. No way could my mission be completed now.

"Nice seeing you again too." I forced a smile. In truth the prince looked drop dead gorgeous. Must be why everyone fangirls over him or the fact that he was *the* prince.

"What are you doing here? Have they already let people in?" He asked. His voice alone caused heat to creep up my cheeks.

"Um." I racked my brain for an excuse but none came.

"Couldn't stay away so you tried finding me?" I made a very unlady like noise and rolled my eyes.

"You wish princeling." I set my face into neutrality as I looked behind me to where the king was. I will never have time to kill him if the prince wouldn't leave. "I have to go." I started to walk back the way I came but before I could the princes hand gripped my arm.

"You didn't answer my question. What are you doing here?" Fear started nibbling at me because I knew he wouldn't let go without an answer.

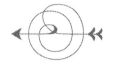

CHAPTER FOUR

Cody

Determination and some thing like fear filled her eyes. Something wasn't right.

"Are you ok?" I desperately wanted to know. I had no idea why I was so interested in her.

"I just remembered mom wanted me to help her with laundry before I went out." I didn't buy that for a minute but I let her go.

"Better hurry then moms can get grouchy." She hurried off without saying bye.

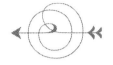

CHAPTER FIVE

Kiera

I took a back route into the servants passages. I wasn't giving up just yet. *Better hurry then moms can get grouchy.* The prince's words echoed in my head. I wouldn't know. My mom ditched me when I was little and I never knew my dad. I was left for Kaden, the most powerful assassin, to raise me. I guess I was lucky in some way, because I knew kids had it worse if left on the streets. I had the luxury of choice even during my missions, for I was Kaden's apprentice and heir.

"Let the party begin!" The King's dreadful voice filled the whole palace. He made it sound like a death sentence and in a way it was.

I peeked through the crack in the wall. I was right behind the throne. *How lucky of me.* Now I just had to find a way to get out of this secret tunnel without being seen. I felt the cracks in the wall. *There.* I felt the handle and slowly slid it open. There was a flimsy see through tapestry over the door so it was easy to sneak behind the throne without being seen. *This was it.* Quickly I rose but before I could slit the king's throat a searing, blinding pain filled my head. Before I could fathom what was happening everything went black.

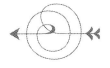

CHAPTER SIX

Cody

I felt the magic as I looked over at my father. Kiera was laying on the floor at his feet. *What did he do?* I ran over to them before anyone noticed and stood where no one could see the girl laying motionless on the ground. The king rarely used his powerful magic, for him to use it now during the biggest party of the year was baffling. *What did she do?* Was my next thought. That's when I saw the blade laying harmlessly at her side. *She tried killing him.* My eyes widened at the prospect. It was extremely bold of her to even try.

"What happened your majesty?" I asked, using my own magic to put an invisible glamour around her.

"Seems like someone wants me dead." He smiled as if that was the most amazing thing in the world. I realized that was the most amazing thing in the world for *him*. Now he had a very good excuse to terrorize his people. It made me down right sick. *He* made me down right sick. I went unnoticed out of the room with Kiera floating beside me. *To the dungeons we go* I thought sadly.

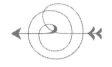

CHAPTER SEVEN

Kiera

I was conscious though I didn't have my eyes open. The air was still, suffocating, I knew I had been caught. Slowly, oh so slowly, I opened my eyes. Panic shot through me. Had I been blinded? I couldn't see a thing. I felt around, careful not to be to noisy. The concrete touch under my fingers gave me a pretty good idea where I was. The dungeon. *Who brought me down here?* I stood up by this time, to my relief, my eyes adjusted to the darkness. *So I wasn't blind* I thought to myself, suddenly calm. I had a grip on the situation now, but for how long?

"Look who's awake." A voice said in the dark. Where the prince's was rich and smooth this one was rough as if the person owning it barely talked.

"What do you want." My eyes narrowed, trying to find where he was.

"You aren't the only one that's good at sneaking around." His voice was everywhere taunting me. I spun around, but soon got too dizzy to stand. I leaned against the wall of my cell, trying hard to keep my bearings. Then a light lit up the space around me, but still no sign of the guy.

"What do you want?" I repeated.

"The question is why do *you* want to kill the king? Someone hire you? Are you a hitman?" I snorted at the word hitman.

"Who wouldn't want to kill the king? I know he treats everyone like shit. He could care less about his people, *sir.*" I spat at him. I knew Kaden would find a way to kill me now that they had me captured. I would welcome the death.

"He treats everyone fairly and don't you so much as doubt that." The guy was in front of me then, to close for comfort. He was guard, but not just a guard he was one of the generals. I was trained to notice the littlest thing so of course I noticed the glint of a lie in his eyes.

"Sorry sir." I would be as cooperative as I could. Pretend that I was merely a subject wanting more than the king offered.

"Who are you?"

"Names Kiera I live in the nearby village and you?" No one knew my real name, only Kaden.

"Josh general of Greenlands Army." The king had many armies in many parts of his kingdom. I would too if I was the most threatened King in existence. "Who hired you?" I scoffed at the question and kept my face neutral.

"No one hired me to do anything. Women get paid nothing if you can't see that." That was the truth in so many ways.

"Why then?" His face was hilarious. I wonder who made him general when he couldn't even keep a straight face.

"We deserve better. Not just women but everyone. Why can't we work equally? Have the same privileges as everyone else? Because you men are so *sexist*." I let emotion show. I've been fighting for *years* to show that women were as amazing as men. That we could even do things better. Like killing.

"That's not tr-" He started to say.

"You can't say nothing if you're not a woman. You will never understand." My voice got rough with emotion. First thing I was taught was how to control my emotions and fake them as well.

Josh, surprisingly, looked like he was going to cry. As if he didn't know.

"Let her out Josh." The Prince's voice came from a darkened corner.

"The king said-"

"*I* said to let her out Josh." Guess I wasn't the only one that was in the habit of interrupting the general.

"Yes sir." He unlocked the door, but didn't hide the fact that his knife was pressed against his side.

I stepped out and nodded my thanks to the prince.

"You can leave." The prince waved his hand in dismissal but didn't keep his eyes off me. Because he didn't trust me? Or was it something else?

"But sir-"

"It's bad enough to question your future king one but twice Josh, really? Leave." Josh glared at both of us before slipping out of the room without another word.

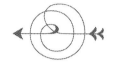

CHAPTER EIGHT

Cody

I had listened to the conversation the whole time and knew what she said was partly true but something wasn't adding up.

"Having fun in the dark?" I grinned.

"You're the one that dragged me down here I'm guessing?" Dodging my question for another one.

I didn't have a choice was what I wanted to say but instead I said. "Yes."

"Figures." She toed the ground but never kept her eyes off of me.

"Who are you really?" If I caught her off guard she didn't show it.

"Keira." I sighed mentally and held out my hand.

"Come on." Was all I said as she grabbed it.

"Where are we going?" I didn't say anything as I led her upstairs and into her new room. I made sure to go slowly so she could remember everything. For some reason I really wanted her to escape with her life and some dignity. I stopped at her dining table and let go of her hand.

"Why did you try to kill my father." I asked, looking down at her. Guilt flashed through her eyes.

"I'm sorry..." Was all she said.

"The only thing I'm sorry about is that you didn't kill him." I turned around and left the explaining up to the servants.

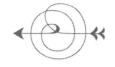

CHAPTER NINE

Keira

It had been a few weeks. The servants came in and out to make sure I had clean clothing, bed sheets, and enough food and water to drink. I hadn't seen the prince since he left me to ponder what he had said. *What did he mean by the only thing I'm sorry about is that you didn't kill him?* I wanted answers. I want to know. I asked the servants for him every day since then and the answer was always no. Josh came in once a day to let me go for a walk wherever I wanted. The only reason I'm alive was because of the prince he kept telling me. I knew that was true and I didn't know what to think about what that meant. Having daydreams about someone having feelings for you was never good to the mind Kaden always said. I had never day dreamed about anyone, ever, so daydreaming about the prince was surprising to me especially since what his father did.

"What are you thinking about?" Josh asked. We were on our daily walk.

"Nothing." He may not be very good at hiding his own feelings but he could read people pretty well.

"You are and aren't a very good liar." I laughed at that.

"What's that supposed to mean?" I shot a grin at him.

"Meaning when you want something accomplished you can keep your face straight. When you think no one's looking you have that distant look on your face and you don't control what people see. It's cute actually." I had never thought about that before and now it gave me something else to work on, but the word cute caught my attention.

"Me? Cute? How?" He laughed and said nothing else during the walk.

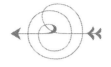

CHAPTER TEN

Josh

I had just dropped Kiera off at her room and was in mine which was only down the hall from her. I picked up my daily report that I had finished this morning when there was a knock on my door.

"Come in!" I knew the prince's knock anywhere we would always sneak into each others rooms at night when we were little.

"Hey Josh." Cody had an urgent look on his face and I motioned for him to sit down. "No thanks but you have to listen to me."

"What's wrong?" I leaned against my desk.

"Father wants you to get close to Kiera and see who she is. Who she really is." He corrected himself. "Don't do it."

"But don't we want to know who she is?" I asked, confused.

"Ok, you and me both know-" I cut him off. Anyone could be listening and I already knew what he was going to say.

"Yes, but it would be good to know." He nodded in understanding.

"How is she?" Something had to have happened between them if he cared so much about her.

"Doing good as far as I can see." He took a deep breath. Relieved or did he want to say something else?

"Don't use her Josh." Was all he said before leaving. I sighed in the silent room. Surely he knew those days were over. Picking up the packet of papers, I walked to the throne room. Kiera had been right. No one liked the king and Cody wasn't the only one that wished she had succeeded.

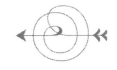

CHAPTER ELEVEN

Cody

I stood next to my father like I did every day. To learn you have to be present was one of father's saying. I could agree on that one thing.

"Here are the reports your majesty." Josh said as he bowed. It made me sick to my stomach that *anyone* had to bow to the monster that called himself king.

"Princeling read this." Was all the king said as he slammed the package of papers into my chest.

"Yes your majesty." He never called me his son and I never called him dad. We've hated each other since I was born. I had many reasons to hate him but what did I do to him? Disappoint him in some way?

"General I need you to do something for me."

"Sir?" Josh asked. He looked completely clueless, I could have hugged him. I only knew some of the plan so I tensed in anticipation to see what he was going to say.

"Pretend to be this Kiera girls friend. Act like you're falling in love with her or anything to make her trust you. Will you do that for me?" Don't let the question fool you. You have two choices. Get killed or do as he says. Prince's are so lucky aren't they?

"Yes sir, anything for you sir." Josh bowed again and left.

"Have those read by tonight princeling." He said in dismissal. I gladly left.

CHAPTER TWELVE

Kiera

Days go past slowly here I realized. Especially when you weren't doing anything all day long. Josh has started coming in more. Talking to me and swapping stories. I've found that I like although I had to make everything up because I would never be able to tell him who I truly am. No one will ever know not even Kaden.

"There has to be more than what you tell me. Come on Kiera just tell me!" Josh and I were sitting under a tree eating apples.

"There is nothing to tell!" I exclaimed. He rolled his eyes in disbelief.

"Surely there is something interesting to tell." He teased.

"Ha! You don't think I'm interesting?" I held my hand close to my heart, pretending to be offended.

"A maid girl living in a close village doing nothing but cleaning all day." He paused to think. "Nope definitely not interesting." He grinned when I playfully slapped his arm. I knew in my heart people that attempted to kill the king wasn't treated this way. There had to be a reason why I wasn't dead because even Prince Cody wouldn't have been able to stop the inevitable.

"Why am I not dead?" I dared whisper. I felt that Josh cared, really cared. I let myself get close to him. I've never been close to anyone. Mom showed me that no one will have a permanent place in your life because they won't stay. Not for you, not for anyone.

A noise sounded to my left and I jumped up into a poised position. A dog was pulling the prince towards us.

"Look who decided to show up." I crossed my arms, mad that the only reason he was here was because of a dog. "Aw who's a cute boy." I knelt down to rub the rottweilers head.

"Thanks." Cody winked down at me, making me roll my eyes.

"Not you idiot." I continued to pet the dog as I glared up at him.

"What's the problem?" He acted so clueless I could have punched him in the face. I looked behind me to where Josh was supposed to be, but he was nowhere in sight.

"You scared him away." I accused.

"You *like* him?" Cody asked looking as if he saw a ghost.

"And what would be wrong with that?" Without permission my voice got defensive.

"N-nothing." He grabbed the dog and quickly walked away. Why were guys so confusing?

CHAPTER THIRTEEN

Cody

I couldn't tell her, if I did I would be in so much trouble. What if he fell for her? I didn't have control of this situation at all. *Father why do you have to put me through so much torture?* Not knowing what to do I headed towards the kennels. Animals always had a way of making me feel better.

"Hey puppy." I knelt down in front of a pen to pet the silky softness of the labrador.

"You like her don't you?" A woman's voice said from behind me. I spun around in surprise.

"Like who?" Kelsey, my sister, had her hands on her hips.

"You know who I'm talking about." I did, but was it that obvious?

"Yea..." No matter what we could always trust each other, because even though she was father's favorite she never trusted him.

"Why don't you tell her?" As though it was that easy. "It is that easy you are just to afraid of being rejected."

"Stop doing that." I hissed. Kelsey had the ability to read minds.

"You take the fun out of everything." She was next to me kneeling in front of the pen by this time. I let myself relax on my heels as I waited for her to give me more sisterly advice. I was only a few years older than her, but she acted so much wiser as if she'd been in this world for hundreds of years. "If you have feelings for her it's only fair for you to tell her. What if she has feelings for you and wants you to make the first move?" She gently pushed my shoulder and stood up. "Think about it, ok bro?" I nodded and waited in silence as she left. What if she's right?

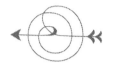

Chapter Fourteen

Kierra

It's been weeks and no sign of Josh. I missed him. A lot. I knew he was probably busy or had gone on a trip. No one told me anything so I was left clueless. It was Sunday morning when I knock sounded at my door. I rushed over and opened it hoping it would be Josh but instead disappointment flooded me when Cody was standing there looking like his princely arrogant self.

"What do you want?" I couldn't keep the snap out of my voice.

"I wanted to tell you that you are invited to the Sunday feast tonight." He looked upset as if my words had hurt him. Good let him be sad like I cared.

"I'm not going." I went to shut the door but his foot stopped it.

"The king *wants* you there." He gently pushed the door open and walked into my room.

"And?" I narrowed my eyes. The prince had the nerve to just walk in my room. Well he had another thing coming. "I don't want you here get out." I pointed towards the door.

"What did I do to you?"

"For one thing you could have let me escape but no you had to lock me in the dungeon! Second you scared Josh off and I haven't seen him since!" I knew my voice was rising and I didn't care. "You probably don't think twice about me so why even come?"

"You're wrong." Was all he said.

"You only came because the king told you to." We stared at each other for a long time before he cleared his throat.

"I volunteered to come because I wanted to see you again. I make sure you have the best care. I ask the servants how you are doing."

"But you can't come yourself."

"Do you know what that would look like?!" He suddenly started yelling. "Father would have your head just because it would look like I had romantic feelings and I for one don't want that to happen."

"Because having romantic feelings for a nobody would look absolutely terrible." His eyes pleaded for me to understand and I did. He didn't want people thinking he would stoop low enough to have feelings for me. "Get out." I stalked to my walk in closet to get ready for the feast.

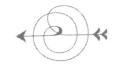

CHAPTER FIFTEEN

Cody

She would never understand the fact that if father found out I had feelings for her he would slowly put an end to her right in front of me. She would never understand that I had slowly been finding little things that made me like her even more. Kierra would never understand that Josh was merely using her.

"Did you tell her?" Kelsey was by my side greeting guests as they filtered in.

"Of course not." I shook one of the royals hands.

"And why not?" She gave me a glare before turning back to the ladies.

"This is not the time to talk about it." I whispered in a warning tone.

"I know." She said and curtsied to another royal.

"I need fresh air." I strode to the closest door and began walking down the silent halls.

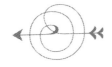

CHAPTER SIXTEEN

Kierra

The food was delicious. The people were nice. Cody and Josh were nowhere to be seen though.

"Hello there!" A girl in a silk black dress stalked towards me as if I were prey waiting to be eaten.

"Hello?" I looked at her without flinching.

"My name is Kelsey." She gave me a big hug, like I was a long lost friend.

"Mine is Kierra." I said, hugging back.

"I know! I'm Cody's sister he doesn't stop talking about you." I raised my eyebrows in surprise. And here I thought he never thought about me twice. "It's true." She giggled.

"May I speak with Lady Kierra." A voice said saving me from saying anything more.

"Of course." She skipped away. A princess indeed.

"Tha-" I started to say before I realized it was Josh. "Oh my god! Where have you been?"

"Can we talk?" I nodded and he led me towards what I thought would be my room but stopped at a door a few rooms away from mine.

"What is this?" I asked as he opened the door.

"My room." He said as I looked around. It was plain. Clearly he didn't stay there often. "It's not fancy but it's good enough." I nodded and looked at him. What did he want to talk about? He sat down on the bed and pulled me close to him. "I was gone on a trip to one of the war camps and I couldn't stop thinking about you."

"Oh." I said lamely. It was all I could come up with.

"I think..." He paused, thinking. "I think I'm in love with you." I stared at him stunned. Could this be real? "Did I say something wrong?" He took my silence as something bad.

"No of course not." I leaned down and kissed him. Slowly at first and then his arms were around me pulling me into his lap.

"I want you..." He mumbled against my lips.

"I want you to." I kissed him harder.

"We should go back before they start asking where we are."

"No!" I said suddenly. "I mean... I want to be here with you."

"Kierra we can't." He was obviously reluctant as I was to leave. We had to leave though.

"I know." I sighed and we walked back to the dining room where the feast was.

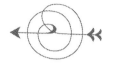

CHAPTER SEVENTEEN

Cody

I had just put all the training equipment up when a door closed.

"Where the hell were you last night?" Kelsey came storming in. Oh she was *pissed*. "Dang right I am you didn't come back! Father was asking for you." She gave me one of her nasty glares.

"I'm sorry, ok? I was going to but you know how much I hate being in crowds." I tried pleading my case but she would have none of that.

"You will be *king* one day. You have to get used this stuff." Her braid had come undone. It only made her look like an angry cat. "This is serious Cody."

"I know Kels." The defeated tone in my voice must have softened her because she was hugging me then. "I don't know if I can do this."

"You will be a great king. Our people will love you."

"They'll see me as him." I ran my hands through my hair in distress. "Power will be the only way I can keep a rebellion from happening."

"That should be your last resort."

"There needs to be someone more suited for this."

"You are very suited. Kings can be nice to, you know." She smiled up at me. She was short and plump. Somehow it made her look older. I loved her to death and if something happened to her I would be lost forever.

"I know. Thank you." She patted my arm and left me to dwell in my thoughts.

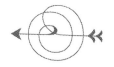

CHAPTER EIGHTEEN

Kierra

It had been days since Josh declared his love for me. Every free moment we had would be together. Dangerously I had been risking telling him things that I swore no one but Kaden would know. I wonder what happened to Kaden anyway. I should be dead somehow but he hadn't poisoned my food or anything. Maybe he thought this was just part of the mission. Who knows?

"So you don't know your parents?" He asked in bewilderment.

"Not really. Promise this stays between us?" Today would be the day I told him everything.

"I promise." I believed him.

"Well I never knew my dad. Mom abandoned me with this guy and I never saw her again. His name is Kaden and he's been training me as an assassin." And so I told him every little detail.

"Wait so you're The Shadow assassin?" His eyes looked as if they would pop out of his head.

"I don't know what they call me." I shrugged because I never listened to the outside world gossip.

"The Shadow assassin is the heir of Kaden the most powerful assassin."

"I guess that would be me then."

"And that is why you tried killing the king?"

"Sort of. What I said when we met is true and that's mostly the reason but yea I got hired to kill him." He kept asking questions for the rest of the day and I answered every one of them truthfully.

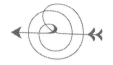

CHAPTER NINETEEN

Cody

I was sitting in my chair in the counsel room. Father had called a meeting for a big party to host the coming princess of Hemmington. Preparing parties was not my cup of tea, but this was one of the many princely duties I have to suffer through.

"You're dismissed." Father said, getting up. *Finally.* I had to see Kierra again, I had to see if she was okay, and I needed to convince her to stay away from Josh.

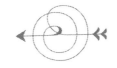

CHAPTER TWENTY

Keirra

I was in my room waiting for Josh to come pick me up for my daily walk. There was a knock on the door, rushing to get to the door I was disappointed to see that it was only Cody.

"Can I help you?" I asked, leaning against the doorway.

"Stay away from Josh please." His voice was desperate, his eyes were pleading.

"Why should I?" I didn't get why he was wanted me to stay away from Josh so badly.

"He isn't what you think."

"I thought you two were friends." I observed him. The nervous shake in his hands were tell tell signs that something was very wrong.

"We were, I mean are, but he's not what you think him to be."

"Why don't you just tell me instead of dance around the problem."

"If I tell you, he'll kill you." With that he strode away. *What is with guys?*

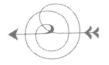

CHAPTER TWENTY ONE

Cody

"What the hell Cody?" Josh pulled me into a servants hallway.

"What?" I kept my face neutral, pretending to not know what he was about to say.

"I was given a job and you are steadily trying to screw it up." He was in my face then.

"Take a step back you're going to make me throw up with your bad breath." Humor always won out, but not this time.

"Stay away from her."

"You don't get to tell me what to do. I am the prince and I am telling you if you hurt her in any way you will be fired on the spot." He took a step back like he had been slapped.

"You love her...." Slow realization dawned in his eyes. I stood there, for once not knowing what to do. I barely knew the girl yet I slowly came to love the little things about her. I stayed in a distance, watching her, trying to keep her safe from Josh. From my father. "Well I have a job to do so please stay out of the way."

"Only if you *promise* not to hurt her." He gave a quick nod.

"Josh the king wants you." One of the guards said. He looked at us strangely, wondering why in the world we were in a servants passage.

"Better hurry up Josh father hates waiting." I said in dismissal. He looked at me to say we weren't finished and walked off.

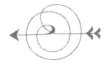

CHAPTER TWENTY TWO

Kierra

I was starting to really hate guys and their vague answers. I waited all day for Josh but there was no sign of him. Surprisingly Cody came back and asked if I'd like to join him for a walk.

"You would like that wouldn't you?" I sneered at him.

"Come on Kier." He displayed his hands in a surrendering motion.

"First of all don't call me that. Second why should I?" My heart stopped when he said my nickname. Jay, my best friend, always called me that.

"You've been cooped up in this room all day. It's not good for you, please come." He was right of course but I was still hesitant.

"Where's Josh?" Hurt flashed in his eyes as if I offended him somehow.

"He had a meeting with father." I sighed and headed out the door.

"Fine but only if you answer everything I ask truthfully."

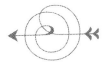

CHAPTER TWENTY THREE

Cody

A few weeks later I was standing in front of father waiting for him to speak.

"What is up with you and this girl?" He finally asked.

"Nothing sir." *What did Josh tell him*?

"Ah, but that is not what the guards have been telling me. Do you have romantic feelings for this girl?"

"No sir. I was just trying to find out why this girl was trying to kill you." I gazed at the wall behind him so he couldn't see the truth hidden in my eyes.

"That is Josh's job not yours." His eyes burned into me.

"I know sir, sorry sir."

"Stay away from this girl." He sounded caring, as if he was worried about her breaking my heart, but I knew there was something more than that.

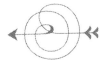

CHAPTER TWENTY FOUR

Kierra

I was reading when Josh sauntered into my room.

"Nice of you to join me." I couldn't help the venom in my voice. It had been five days since I last saw him. Prince Cody had kept me company during that time. Surprisingly I had come to enjoy it, even looked forward to it.

"I have been busy." Was all he said as he stared at me.

"What?"

"You're beautiful." His voice was hushed as he walked towards me.

"I-I'm not" I stammered.

"You are." He picked me up and started laying me on the bed.

"What are you d-doing?" I had a really good idea and I feared he would hate me once he saw me naked.

"Making sure you get the love you deserve." Kissing my neck as he slid his hand up my shirt, I shivered at the attention. Never before had I experienced this kind of attention.

"Josh..." My shirt came off and he stared at all of the scars covering my body.

"Where did you get those?" His face twisted in anger. Little did he know I had continuously cut myself when I was younger. These scars were intentional.

"I used to self harm..." My voice cracked. Hate was all I saw in those beautiful eyes. "Please Josh." I haven't cried in a long time but tonight was the exception.

"You filthy attention seeking *whore*." Tears streamed down my cheeks as he stormed out. I tried following, but fell in the hallway. I was to weak to stand or to care that I was in a palace hallway without a shirt on.

"Kier are you ok?" The prince's voice came from behind me. I didn't have time to answer as he scooped me up in his arms and closed the door to my bedroom.

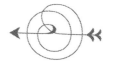

CHAPTER TWENTY FIVE

Cody

I had watched Josh storm out of Kierra's room, had watched her stumble after him. My heart tore to pieces that he would leave her in that position. She was shirtless so I quickly wrapped a blanket around her to keep her warm.

"Kierra what's wrong?" I asked for about the tenth time. She had gone into shock and hadn't answered me. *What happened?*

"He's going to tell the king everything isn't he?" I slowly nodded. "That's what you were trying to warn me about?" I nodded again. She laughed humorlessly. "Why couldn't you have just told me? Why did you let him do this to me?" She had suddenly gone hoarse. My breathing hitched. *Why didn't i?* A voice whispered to me, *because you're scared of your father.*

"My father doesn't have a good side it's all bad. I wish I was never born into this family, all I've ever wanted was a loving mother and father. He has spies all around the castle. If they found out I had told you they would have killed you."

"Maybe that wouldn't be such a bad thing." Her voice was clipped.

"What happened?" I asked again.

"He said he loved me a few days ago and hadn't seen him until a few minutes ago. He said I was beautiful, of course I believed him, he was undressing me when he saw the scars."

"Scars?" She sighed, using her hand to prop her head up.

"Josh is already going to tell King Austin I guess there's is no point in hiding my story now." I waited for her to go on. "I never knew my father and I was young when my mom gave me away to the master of assassins. I never knew why she would give me away to an assassin. Kaden's like a father to me. He trained me to survive. He means good we only kill the really bad people and your father ended up on that list. I am one of the best so I volunteered. I didn't succeed obviously." She laughed humorlessly again.

"Come on I want to show you something." I waved for her to put the shirt back on while waiting at the door. Within a few seconds she was at my side and we were headed down towards the training field.

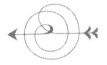

CHAPTER TWENTY SIX

Kierra

"Where are going?" I asked. I hadn't really felt like going anywhere but I knew I had to have a much needed walk.

"You'll see." In a span of 5 minutes Cody had become my closest friend. Maybe I had only craved companionship when I met Josh so I didn't see the signs that he wasn't true to the heart. I fell for it and now I was paying the consequences. "Here we are." We were in a meadow but instead of flowers, training equipment covered the open space. A gasp escaped my lips. I missed the knives in my hands, the arrows flying from the bow.

"Is this a trick?" I had to ask. He shook his head and walked towards the rack with numerous weapons. "You trust me?" He glanced at me with a small smile on his lips.

"Well Mrs. Shadow Assassin I would do anything to get this kingdom in better hands." He winked as if allowing the murder of his own father was completely normal. I grabbed a swords and swung it around to check its balance.

"Perfect." I murmured.

"Let's see what you got." Before I could barely deflect the oncoming attack he swung at me. He smirked as he swung again. *Oh this was going to be fun.*

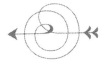

CHAPTER TWENTY SEVEN

Cody

By the light dancing in her eyes and her swift feet I knew Kierra enjoyed herself while training maybe even while killing. We talked all throughout our training session and kept talking as we walked back to her room. I didn't comment on the fact that she hid a dagger in her jeans. I could only hope it was for my father and not for me.

"I've been looking for you." A booming voice carried down the hall. Father was standing at *her* door waiting for *me*.

"Oh?" I didn't allow my shock to show. I felt Kierra stiffen beside me, that was the only hint she showed of her terror.

"Kill her." Everything became slow. Josh *slowly* lunged toward Kierra as she *slowly* lunged towards father. My power flared as everyone but Kierra and I froze. Kierra's dagger embedded itself in the king's heart. My knife slit my old best friends throat as I unfreeze the world.

"You can do that?!" Her eyes were wide in wonder, not fear. I nodded. I never talked about my powers. "Wow."

"Cody..." Kelsey walked toward us.

"Kels I'm sor-"

"Don't be I can't wait for your crowning ceremony!"

"The story is someone unknown had killed the king and general as we happened to pass by." They both nodded. I had nothing to worry about.

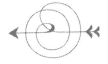

CHAPTER TWENTY EIGHT

Kierra

It had been months since the prince was crowned king. Life had more or less went back to normal. The assassins were now allies with the king and I was back to killing. Kaden had explained that he loved me too much to kill me and everyone had accepted his decision that if I exposed them they would go into hiding. Luckily it never came to that.

One Saturday night I was going into a bar when someone grabbed my arm. "Walk with me?" Cody's honey sweet voice said.

"It would be my pleasure." I bowed and walked next to him.

"How is life?" He asked as I glanced up at the night sky.

"As normal as assassin's lives are I guess." I had slowly gotten over the pain that Josh had caused me. I didn't feel satisfaction over his death. I had felt hollow, but the new kings precedence always made things brighter for me.

"Ah, yes." He mockingly bowed. "Your highness, princess of assassins." I pushed him away none too gently.

"Call me Haley." I knew I could trust him. I also knew I should guard my heart before it completely broke but there was no guarding it from this guy.

"So you finally come out about your real name."

"Yep." We walked in silence for a while before he said, "It's a nice name." I smiled warmly.

"I think we will become very close one day." The lights brightened as I realized what true love actually was.

Printed in the United States
By Bookmasters